Mr. and Mrs. God in the Creation Kitchen

For Richard Erdoes
N. W.

For my wife, Jen—your amazing love, knowledge, and adoration
of children is, in so many ways, an inspiration to us all.
Thanks, Mom and Dad, for making all of us.
To the imaginative Rachael, Noah, and Bisk, and of course to the
main ingredients for great book-making, Karen Lotz and Chris Paul.
T. B. E.

Text copyright © 2006 by Nancy Wood
Illustrations copyright © 2006 by Timothy Basil Ering

First edition 2006

Library of Congress Cataloging-in-Publication Data is available.

Library of Congress Catalog Card Number 2005053187

ISBN 0-7636-1258-8

2 4 6 8 10 9 7 5 3

Printed in China

This book was typeset in Poliphilus.
The illustrations were done in ink and acrylic.

Candlewick Press
2067 Massachusetts Avenue
Cambridge, Massachusetts 02140

visit us at www.candlewick.com

Mr. and Mrs. God in the Creation Kitchen

Nancy Wood

illustrated by

Timothy Basil Ering

CANDLEWICK PRESS
CAMBRIDGE, MASSACHUSETTS

Deep in the heavens, in a space without beginning or end, was the Creation Kitchen. In it were all kinds of pots and pans, jars and mixing bowls, and an oven big enough to roast a star.

Off in a corner, Mr. and Mrs. God were hard at work. Fans were going. Something very large and round was baking in the oven. When the timer rang, Mr. God opened the oven door and let the giant orb roll itself out into the universe. It was the brightest, hottest thing either one of them had ever seen.

"I'm going to call it the sun," Mr. God said.

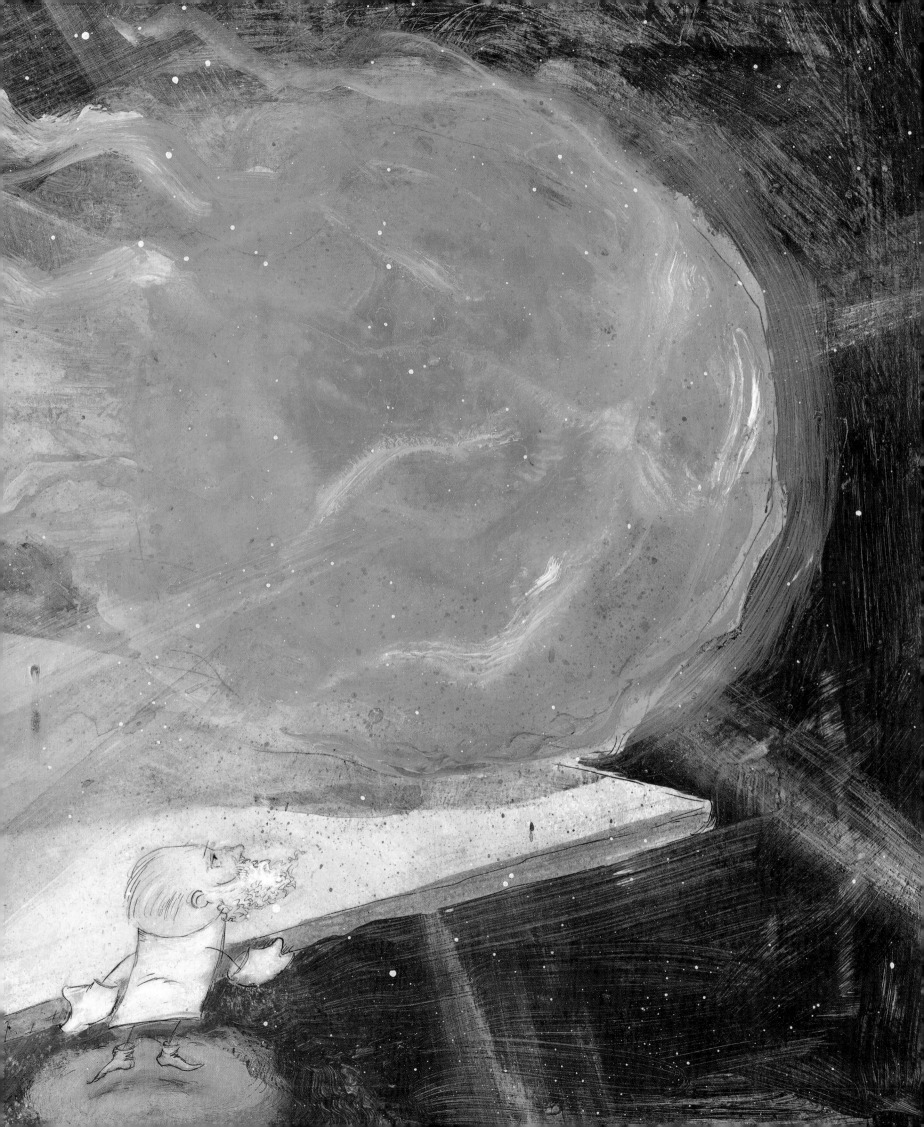

Mrs. God started molding another fat lump of dough. She baked it slowly, peeking in the oven every so often to see if it was done. "Not yet," she said. "But soon."

When it was ready, she flung the fiery ball out into space. "There," she said. "I'm naming that one Earth."

Earth was boiling hot. "You made it," said Mr. God. "You cool it off."

Mrs. God whipped together some clouds and poured them over the glowing ball. At last it began to turn blue.

Mr. God stuck his finger in the crust to see how it was coming along. "Not bad," he said. "Maybe I'll make some creatures to go with it."

Mr. God knew the creatures had to be something you'd notice. Something big. Something with a terrible noise. He looked through all the boxes in the pantry to find just the right ingredients. Growls and roars. Sharp teeth. Huge feet. "I've got it," he said.

Mr. God worked until his new creature was finished. Then he pushed it over the edge of the Creation Kitchen and down onto the earth.

Oh my! It was bigger than he'd meant it to be. After he'd made a few more, he called to Mrs. God. "Look down there. How do you like them?"

Mrs. God was quite upset. The enormous, ghastly things had the biggest tails imaginable. "They're hideous," she said. "What were you thinking?"

Mr. God looked down at his creatures. They were rather unattractive. He wished he could take them back, but they had already made some baby monsters, and the baby monsters had made even more monsters.

"Maybe they were a mistake," said Mr. God.
"What can I do?" He grabbed a red-hot coal
from the oven and flung it down.

"It's time for something beautiful," said Mrs. God. She looked around. She took several handfuls of fins and tails from the boxes. Then she got a big bowl and filled it with all the colors she loved. Next she mixed it all together and emptied the bowl into the bluest waters on Earth. "Perfect," she said. "Come see."

Mr. God was working on something of his own. "Look at that beak!" he shouted. He stood back and admired what he'd made. Then the creature spread its wings and flew off. Straight down to the ocean it went. It ate up Mrs. God's pretty swimming creatures in one big gulp.

"How could you?" she said to Mr. God.

Mrs. God did not speak to Mr. God for a thousand years.
Mr. God wondered what he could do to please her.

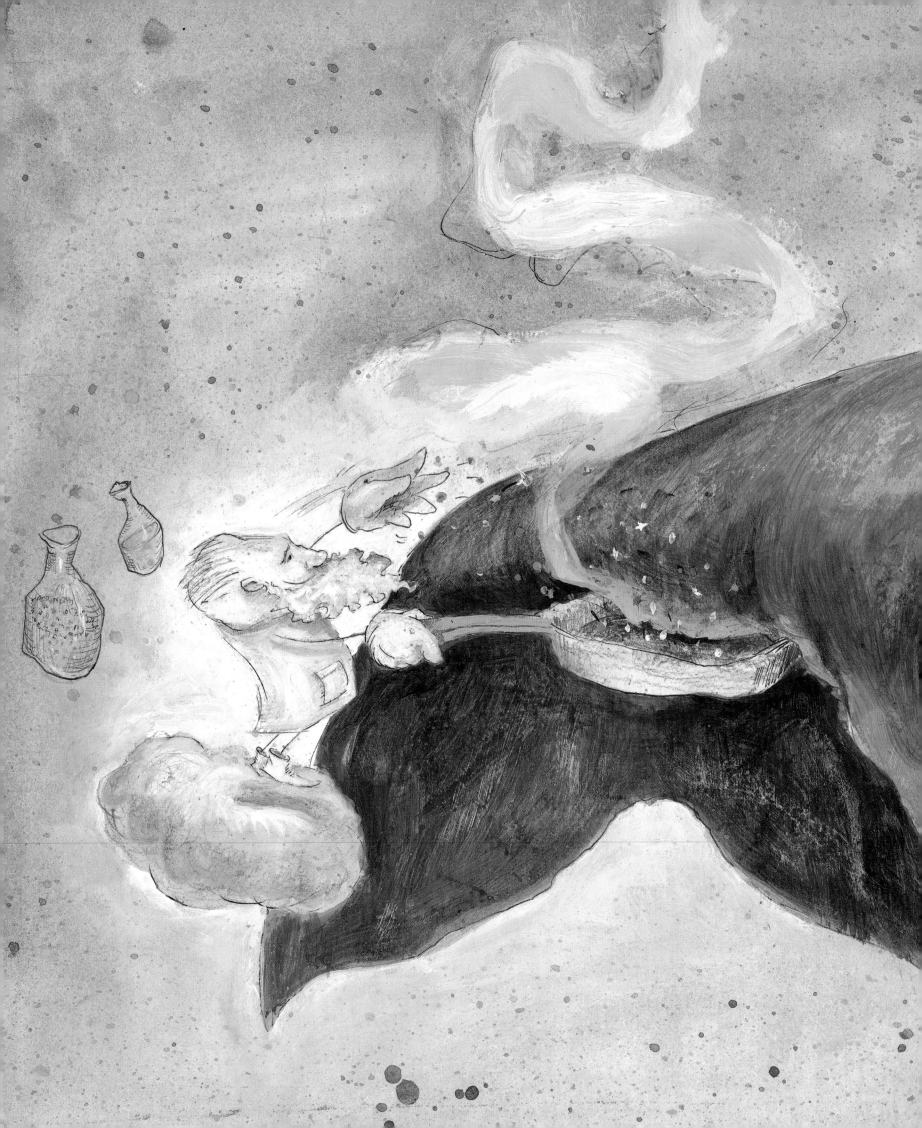

Finally he took an enormous pile of clay and made the biggest creature yet. He had a hard time getting it into the frying pan. Its tail hung out.

The creature cooked for a long time until it was done. Then Mr. God dragged it out and stood in its wide-open mouth. "Oh my," he said.

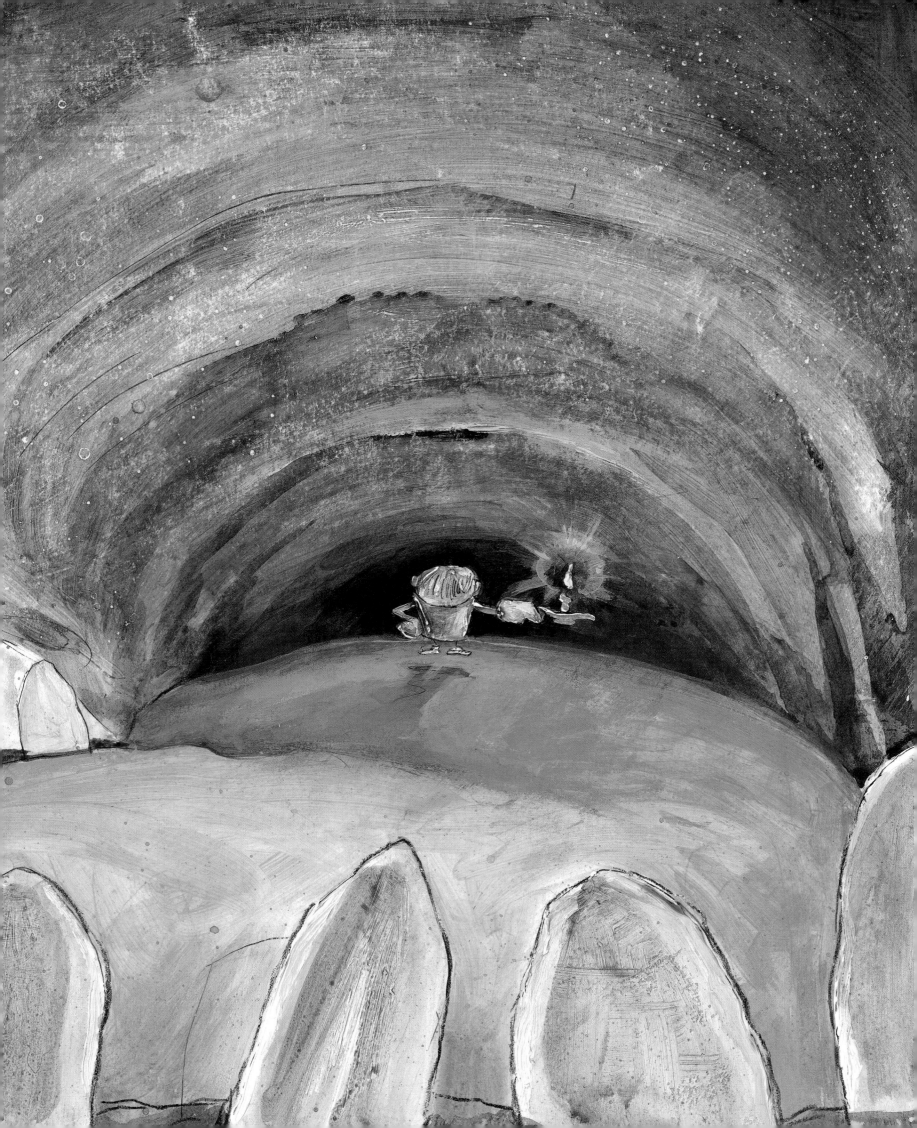

Mr. God pushed the creature into the ocean. Mrs. God heard the splash and went over to take a closer look.

"You have created a masterpiece," she said. "A little large, but it has character." Mrs. God had forgiven Mr. God at last.

Pretty soon all the rest of the creatures were made.
It had taken a long time, but Mr. and Mrs. God were
pleased with the results.

"We forgot something," Mr. God said. He took a leftover piece of clay and rolled it out, giving it arms and legs and a head. At the last minute, he added a neck.

"What are they?" asked Mrs. God, who was working on a second one.

"Who knows?" said Mr. God. He glued on hair and toes. Eyeballs and ears.

They baked the two creatures in the oven at a low temperature. When the creatures looked as if they were ready, Mr. and Mrs. God set them down on Earth.

"I wonder how they'll turn out," said Mr. God.
"Who knows?" said Mrs. God.
"We'll just have to wait and see."